The Sick-in-Bed Birthday

Story by Linda Wagner Tyler

Pictures by Susan Davis

Viking Kestrel

VIKING KESTREL
Published by the Penguin Group
Viking Penguin Inc., 40 West 23rd Street, New York, New York 10010, U.S.A.
Penguin Books Ltd, 27 Wrights Lane, London W8 5TZ England
Penguin Books Australia Ltd, Ringwood, Victoria, Australia
Penguin Books Canada Ltd, 2801 John Street, Markham, Ontario, Canada L3R 1B4
Penguin Books (N.Z.) Ltd, 182-190 Wairau Road, Auckland 10, New Zealand

Penguin Books Ltd, Registered Offices: Harmondsworth, Middlesex, England

First published in 1988 by Viking Penguin Inc.
Published simultaneously in Canada
Text copyright © Linda Wagner Tyler, 1988
Illustrations copyright © Susan Davis, 1988
All rights reserved

Library of Congress Cataloging in Publication Data
Tyler, Linda Wagner.
The sick-in-bed birthday/by Linda Wagner Tyler; illustrated by Susan Davis.
p. cm.
Summary: When the nurse sends Tucky Pig home from school on the
day of his birthday party, he is convinced that this will be the
worst birthday he's ever had.
ISBN 0-670-81823-2
[1. Pigs—fiction.   2. Birthdays—Fiction.   3. Sick—fiction.]
I. Davis, Susan, 1948- ill.   II. Title.
PZ7. T94Si   1988
[E]—dc 19   (87-32617)
Color separations by Imago Ltd., Hong Kong
Printed in Hong Kong by South China Printing Company
Set in Souvenir Light
1   2   3   4   5   92   91   90   89   88

Last Friday was my birthday.

It was also the saddest day of my life.

The day before, Mom and I made cupcakes
to bring to school.

I decorated each one differently for everyone
in my class.

We even went to the bakery and ordered a cake
for after school.

My two best friends were going to sleep over.

But when I woke up on my birthday, I didn't feel
very well. I didn't tell Mom and I went to
school anyway.

When I got to school I felt sick. I couldn't even
eat my cupcake. My teacher, Mrs. O'Connell,
took me to the nurse's office.

The nurse took my temperature.

"Hmmm," she said. "I'm going to call your mom."

Then she covered me up with a blanket, and I thought about my own cozy bed and soft quilt.

I tried to sleep and not to cry.

I was really glad when Mom finally came
to take me home.

I couldn't even stay awake in the car.

Mom helped me put on my pajamas. "Oh no," she said.

"You have red spots all over your stomach."

Mom called the doctor and told me the news.

"The doctor says you have chicken pox!"

"Can Beatie and Zeff still sleep over?" I asked.

Mom said, "No, because they might get sick too."

Dad brought home some medicine to stop
the itching. He said he was sorry my friends
couldn't sleep over. He promised we would all do
something really special when I felt better.

Before I went to sleep, Mom and Dad brought me

my favorite ice cream and even sang

"Happy Birthday."

The next day I had even more spots
but I felt better, so Mom let me
go downstairs to watch T.V.

Zeff called and said he'd give me my present

when he was able to come over.

Beatie sent me a drawing.

On Tuesday the mailman brought a bag
of mail just for me. Everyone in my class
had made me a card!

I hung the one from Mrs. O'Connell right
over my bed.

All week long Mom and I played games and thought

of fun things we might do with Beatie and Zeff.

Finally I was better and Beatie and Zeff could come over.

We had so much fun. It was a birthday worth waiting

or thanks to Mom and Dad and my friends.